Mega Movie Stars

By Riley Brooks

Scholastic Inc.

New York Toronto London Auckland

Sydney Mexico City New Delhi Hong Kong

© 2010 by Scholastic

ISBN 978-0-545-22542-7

Published by Scholastic Inc.
SCHOLASTIC and associated logos are trademarks and/or registered trademarks of Scholastic Inc.

12 11 10 9 8 7 6 5 4 3 2 1   10 11 12 13 14 15/0

Designed by Deena Fleming
Printed in the U.S.A.   40
First printing, June 2010

There is nothing quite like the magic of the movies. Everyone loves getting a big, buttery tub of popcorn, settling back into a cushy seat, and watching as the lights go down and you can escape into the story on the big screen in front of you. Lots of things have to come together to create the perfect movie—a great script, a killer soundtrack, and, of course, super-hot stars! This year's biggest blockbuster hits are filled with the hottest stars around, and we've got all of the info on your fave actors! So pop some popcorn, grab a soda, and curl up with this book to learn all about this year's coolest silver screen stars! You might be surprised to find out that most of them are a lot like you!

A TEAM

This big screen version of the 1980's hit television show gets an A+ from fans! As do its handsome stars—Bradley Cooper, Liam Neeson, Quinton "Rampage" Jackson, and newcomer Sharlto Copley. Here are the fast facts on these cuties!

Bradley Cooper

HOMETOWN: Jenkintown, Pennsylvania

BIRTHDAY: January 5, 1975

MOST FAMOUS FILMS: Wedding Crashers, Failure to Launch, Yes Man, He's Just Not That Into You, The Hangover, All About Steve, The Comebacks, The Rocker

PREVIOUS TELEVISION SHOWS: Alias, Kitchen Confidential, Jack & Bobby, Miss Match, Nip/Tuck

HOBBIES: hiking, jogging, cooking

FAVORITE FOOD: Italian food

Quinton "Rampage" Jackson

HOMETOWN: Memphis, Tennessee

BIRTHDAY: June 20, 1978

MOST FAMOUS FILMS: Confessions of a Pit Fighter, Bad Guys, The Midnight Meat Train

TELEVISION GUEST ROLE: The King of Queens

OTHER JOB: UFC Ultimate Fighter

HOBBIES: Mixed Martial Arts

Liam Neeson

HOMETOWN: Ballymena, Northern Ireland

BIRTHDAY: June 7, 1952

MOST FAMOUS FILMS: *Schindler's List; Les Misérables; The Haunting; Star Wars: Episode I The Phantom Menace; Gangs of New York; Love Actually; The Chronicles of Narnia: The Lion, the Witch and the Wardrobe; Batman Begins; The Chronicles of Narnia: Prince Caspian; The Chronicles of Narnia: Voyage of the Dawn Treader*

TELEVISION GUEST ROLES: *The Simpsons, Saturday Night Live*

HOBBIES: soccer

CHILDREN: sons Micheál, age 15, and Daniel, age 14

Sharlto Copley

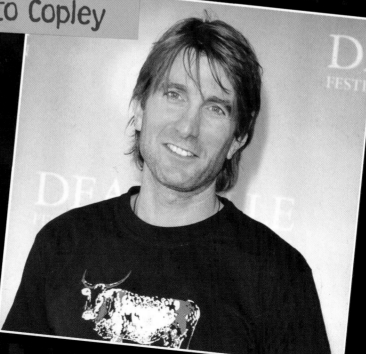

HOMETOWN: Johannesburg, South Africa

BIRTHDAY: November 27, 1973

PREVIOUS FILMS: *Alive in Joburg, District 9*

OTHER JOBS: screenwriter, director, producer

HOBBIES: watching movies, making short films with his friends

Alice in Wonderland

Director Tim Burton has breathed new life into this classic tale by spicing it up with his signature dark sense of humor and breathtaking style. He cast some of his favorite stars in key roles, like Johnny Depp as the Mad Hatter, Anne Hathaway as the White Queen, and Helena Bonham Carter as the Red Queen. For the key role of Alice, Tim cast up-and-coming Australian starlet Mia Wasikowska, and the Aussie beauty is sure to blow Hollywood away with this performance! So what was it like for these stars to take on such beloved characters?

JOHNNY DEPP

on what influenced his version of the Mad Hatter:

"**WELL,** certainly the book. The book has a basis for everything. There are little mysteries, little clues in the book that I found fascinating, that were keys to at least my understanding of the Mad Hatter, like him saying, 'I'm investigating things that begin with the letter M.' That was huge for me, because when you do a little digging, you realize you're talking about a hatter, a man who made hats, and you go back and look at some of the history. 'Hatters' — there's the term that this guy or that guy is 'mad as a hatter.' There was reason for that, and the reason for that was mercury poisoning. They got mercury poisoning because there was mercury in the glue. So they start to go a little sideways. So I found out what the 'M' was and why they went nuts. So that became a huge thing."

anne Hathaway
on filming as the White Queen:

"I PLAY the White Queen. I filmed this past fall. I worked for two weeks. I had an absolute ball. I was very lucky I had a couple of weeks to create this character. The thing about Tim is that, whenever you are working with an auteur like that, your limits for the character are the limits for their imagination and in the case of Tim Burton there are no limits to his imagination. It was wonderful living in a very creative world every day; it was odd. I have never done full greenscreen before: There was a room four times the size of this room, with ceilings [that] go three times as high and it's all green. You feel like you live in a kind of ant colony… a very green one. That was strange… but it was just new. I loved working with Johnny Depp. And Mia, the girl who plays Alice — people are gonna love her portrayal; she is a very exciting young actress… I loved it. I just loved playing my character."

mia wasikowska
on working with Tim Burton:

"I'M FILMING *Alice in Wonderland* at the moment, which is wonderful, with Tim Burton. And I really admire him as a film-maker, so it's just so much fun to be working with him. Yeah, it's been great. Every day is something different. I'm learning things every day."

Avatar:
The Last Airbender

Avatar: The Last Airbender has been a favorite with kids (and parents!) everywhere as an animated show on Nickelodeon. But it hit the big screen as a suspenseful live-action adventure re-imagined by famed director M. Night Shyamalan. Of course, he picked several total cuties to bring the characters to life including *Twilight* alum Jackson Rathbone, Dev Patel, and Noah Ringer. It was a lot of pressure for the actors to bring those animated characters to life on the big screen, but they did it!

JACKSON RATHBONE
on preparing for his role:

"**I'VE BEEN** training in various styles of Kung Fu since December, and I love it! It connects the body and mind in a way a textbook could never achieve...I can kill from 10 feet away with a spear...Purty sweeeeeetttt..."

DEV PATEL
on his character, Zuko:

"**ZUKO** is a boy, and he's struggling to impress his father and trying to get his honor and love back," remarks Patel. "And then there's Shaun Toub, who plays my uncle, and who treats Zuko like a son. Like in life, you take your anger out on the people you love the most, and Zuko sort of neglects his uncle because he's on this one-track mission to find this boy. It makes it really interesting. They have a good dynamic: This naïve boy who acts on aggression all of the time, and then you have this wise, older uncle who is like the calm within the storm. It's a good dynamic."

NOAH RINGER
on nabbing the part of Aang:

"**I KNEW** about the cartoon three years before. Ever since I've been shaving my head, everybody has called me Aang. I watched the show because everybody would tell me, 'You have to watch this cartoon. He looks just like you!' The movie is definitely different [from the TV series], but if we would've done the same thing as the cartoon, what would be exciting about that? It's fun to change that and do something new."

The Twilight Saga: Eclipse

The Twilight Saga movies have been hits with fans of the books around the world. And that's in a large part thanks to its super-hot stars. Whether you're on Team Jacob or Team Edward, all fans can agree that the actors and actresses are all serious hotties! Of course, *Eclipse* is no exception! The third movie in the saga is full of romantic moments, dangerous action, and plenty of screen time for all of your fave stars! Here are the facts every Twi-hard must know!

Kristen Stewart

BIRTHDAY: April 9, 1990

HOMETOWN: Los Angeles, California

BIG BREAK: *Panic Room*

NEXT PROJECT: *K-11*

FAMILY: parents John and Jules Stewart, and three brothers Cameron, Dana, and Taylor

PETS: three dogs Oz, Jack, and Lily, and a cat Jella

HOBBIES: reading, surfing, playing guitar, writing, going to concerts

FAVORITE FOOD: apples and sushi

FAVORITE MOVIE: *The Shining*

FAVORITE BOOK: *East of Eden* and *Cannery Row* by John Steinbeck, and *The Stranger* by Albert Camus

FAVORITE COLOR: blue

BIRTHDAY: May 13, 1986
HOMETOWN: London, England
CURRENT RESIDENCE: Los Angeles, California
BIG BREAK: *Harry Potter and the Goblet of Fire*
FAMILY: parents Clare and Richard Pattinson, and two older sisters, Lizzy and Victoria
PETS: a dog named Patty
HOBBIES: playing guitar and piano
FAVORITE FOOD: cheeseburgers
FAVORITE MOVIE: *The Exorcist* and *One Flew Over the Cuckoo's Nest*
FAVORITE COLOR: gray

Robert Pattinson

Taylor Lautner

BIRTHDAY: February 11, 1992
HOMETOWN: Grand Rapids, Michigan
CURRENT RESIDENCE: Los Angeles, California
BIG BREAK: *The Adventures of Sharkboy and Lavagirl*
FAMILY: parents Dan and Deborah Lautner, and little sister Makena
PETS: a maltese dog named Roxy
HOBBIES: extreme martial arts, football, baseball
FAVORITE FOOD: steak
FAVORITE MOVIE: *Accepted*
FAVORITE BOOKS: the Twilight series
FAVORITE COLOR: baby blue

FLiPPeD

Based on novel by Wendelin Van Draanen, *Flipped* is the love story of two teen-agers, Juli and Bryce, who have known each other since they were seven. Juli is played by smart and sassy Madeline Carroll, and Bryce is played by mega-cutie Callan McAuliffe. Both Madeline and Callan are poised to step into the Holly-wood spotlight as *Flipped* premieres—so watch out for more from them soon!

MEET MADELINE:

Madeline Carroll is only fourteen years old, but she's already booked more jobs than many adult actresses. She was born on March 18, 1996 and raised in sunny Los Angeles, California. Madeline began modeling when she was three years old. Her first job was a Sears catalog! Shortly after, Madeline was discovered by her theatrical agent in a nail salon and was soon booking commercials and small roles in television shows including *Cold Case*, *Grey's Anatomy*, *Lie to Me*, *Wanted*, and *Lost*. She's also appeared in movies like *The Santa Clause 3: The Escape Clause* and *Resident Evil: Extinction*.

Madeline got her first real big break starring alongside Kevin Costner in 2008's *Swing Vote*. She told collider.com, "When I first got the lines for *Swing Vote*, I loved the script. I loved everything about it, I loved the character." She followed *Swing Vote* with the role of Nikki in *Vanilla Gorilla* and providing a voice for 2009's *Astro Boy*. Then she landed the lead role in *The Spy Next Door* alongside Jackie Chan and Alina Foley. But the film she has been most looking forward to is *Flipped* with adorable co-star Callan McAuliffe. When

Madeline isn't acting, she's usually playing with her three brothers and her dog named Spot.

MADELINE CARROL

CUTIE CALLAN:

Callan McAuliffe is a fifteen-year-old Australian native who is just beginning to make his mark in Hollywood. The Sydney stud has been acting since he was eight, but has only recently gained notoriety. He has since booked an agent in Los Angeles. "There was a unique quality about his acting that just came across as extremely natural and extremely confident, but not in a cocky way," Callan's agent, Nicholas Bogner, told *The Sydney Morning Herald*.

Callan had a small recurring role on the Australian hit television show *Packed to the Rafters* and then began booking film gigs. He has landed starring roles in two Australian movies: *Resistance* and *Franswa Sharl*. But, despite his success, Callan remains very down to earth. "My mum mostly drives me around and organizes auditions," Callan told *The Manly Daily*. "If I get a part I go to work on the set and then I come home. It's pretty normal." Of course, his friends at school aren't always quite so laid back about Callan's stardom. "The guys at school kind of tease me but I don't really care. They're all my mates. The school has been really supportive," Callan explained to *The Manly Daily*. His mates back in Australia are sure to have something to say about Callan getting to work with beautiful Madeline in *Flipped*!

The Green Horne

Not all superheroes are serious crime-fighters! Seth Rogen has turned t
classic character of the Green Hornet into a hilarious, joke-cracking po
house with Jay Chou along as his giggle-inducing sidekick Kato. Seth is
writing the movie with Evan Goldberg, so he's been getting into charac
for quite a while!

Seth R

On trying a different approach to a superhero movie:

"Just a few weeks ago, [co-writer Evan Goldberg and I] laid out our outline for the movie to the studio, and before the phone call, Evan and I were like, 'This is not like any superhero movie — they might just hate that. It's not using any of the normal superhero movie formats.... It's more like a regular action movie.' [But] they really liked it and told us to go for it."

On making *The Green Hornet* funny:

"There's a more comedic version and a less comedic version, and we don't know what will feel right until we're actually writing it."

On finding the right Kato:

"It's a very intense action movie and the relationship between Green Hornet and Kato, a lot of comedy comes from that. At first actually, we weren't even sure going in [if] [h]e could be more of a Jet Li-type guy who maybe isn't the funniest guy in the world, but he's physically very impressive, or whether it would be more of a Stephen Chow-type guy who can do martial arts, but clearly has a sense of humor. In the version that we've made it seems like a Stephen Chow-type guy would be more suitable for the role."

On possibly disappointing die-hard *Green Hornet* fans:

"You know, we're not trying to make what they would probably consider to be a 100 percent safe version of a movie like this. We like to push the envelope in some directions. We like to do things that we find interesting and new and original."

GULLIVER'S TRAVELS

No family vacation was ever this much fun! When wannabe travel writer Gulliver sets off into the Bermuda Triangle, he has no idea that he's going to be shipwrecked on an island full of tiny people! Always hilarious, Jack Black plays goofy Gulliver with his usual laugh-out-loud style. Here are all the key facts about your fave *Gulliver* stars!

Jack Black

BIRTHDAY: August 28, 1969

HOMETOWN: San Monica, California

CURRENT RESIDENCE: Los Angeles, California

BIG BREAK: High Fidelity

BIGGEST MOVIES: Kung Fu Panda, Tropic Thunder, The Holiday, King Kong, School of Rock, Be Kind Rewind, Ice Age, Shallow Hal, Enemy of the State, Mars Attacks!, The Cable Guy, Demolition Man

HEIGHT: 5'6"

HOBBIES: playing music with his band Tenacious D, collecting coins

FAVORITE BAND: Urge Overkill

Emily Blunt

BIRTHDAY: February 23, 1983
HOMETOWN: London, England
CURRENT RESIDENCE: Los Angeles, California
BIG BREAK: *My Summer of Love*
BIGGEST MOVIES: *The Devil Wears Prada, The Jane Austen Book Club, Dan in Real Life, Charlie Wilson's War, The Great Buck Howard, Sunshine Cleaning*
HEIGHT: 5'7"
HOBBIES: singing, playing cello, horseback riding
FAVORITE FOOD: Auntie Anne's Pretzels
FAVORITE TV SHOW: *The Office*

Jason Segal

BIRTHDAY: January 18, 1980
HOMETOWN: Los Angeles, California
BIG BREAK: *Freaks and Geeks*
BIGGEST MOVIES: *I Love You, Man; Knocked Up; Forgetting Sarah Marshall; Slackers; Dead Man on Campus; Can't Hardly Wait*
HEIGHT: 6'4"
HOBBIES: basketball, playing piano, writing songs and movies
FAVORITE MOVIE: *The Muppet Movie*
FAVORITE TV SHOW: *Little Britain*

Harry Potter
and the Deathly Hallows:
Part 1

The much beloved Harry Potter series is coming to a close—and its stars are now all grown-up! Emma, Daniel, and Rupert have grown from adorable kids into mega-hot actors before our very eyes. Now these sizzling stars are moving on to new projects, higher education, and some romance of their own! But how do these big stars feel about saying good-bye to these roles?

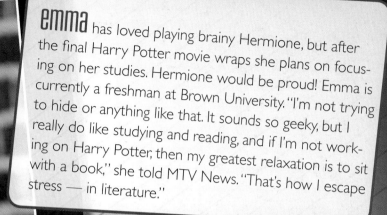

emma has loved playing brainy Hermione, but after the final Harry Potter movie wraps she plans on focusing on her studies. Hermione would be proud! Emma is currently a freshman at Brown University. "I'm not trying to hide or anything like that. It sounds so geeky, but I really do like studying and reading, and if I'm not working on Harry Potter, then my greatest relaxation is to sit with a book," she told MTV News. "That's how I escape stress — in literature."

Emma Watson

Of course, if the right part comes along Emma might be willing to work acting into her academic schedule. "If it was something I really wanted to do, then I wouldn't say no. But at the same time I've been working solidly since I was, like, 10... so I'm going to take a bit of break," she explained to MTV News. But Emma won't be able to stay away from acting forever. She loves it too much. She's already signed on to star in 2010's *Napoleon and Betty*. And, after she finishes college, she'll probably be back to wowing us on the silver screen full time with her fantastic acting chops. At least we hope that's what happens!

Daniel Radcliffe

UNLIKE Emma, Daniel isn't interested in taking time off from acting after *Harry* wraps up. "...I certainly do need to establish with people and within the industry the fact that I absolutely want to make a career out of this and that I'd never be content with just coasting along on the Harry Potter fame. That's what motivates me. I get a huge kick out of doing good work and out of working on different films with different crews, so hopefully that's what these films will achieve. That said, I'd never want to distance myself from Harry Potter because I'm incredibly proud of the films and, particularly with the fifth one, proud of what I did in it. It's not a question of absolutely detaching myself from it, but rather establishing myself as an actor rather than a character."

Daniel has used his time recently between Harry Potter films to try his hand at different acting opportunities. He starred in the play *Equus* on Broadway and wowed critics with his mature performance He filmed a made-for-television movie called *My Boy Jack* about the relationship between famed writer Rudyard Kipling and his son, Jack. Then he filmed the small, independent film *December Boys* in Australia. Daniel is psyched for fans to see him play something different and he hopes his latest projects will be hits with fans. In the meantime he's looking for films that will challenge him. He also hopes to make a return to Broadway in the next two or three years. He's even taking tap lessons to prepare. He told *New York Magazine*, "So far it's just a bit of shuffling... If I do a musical I want to be proper! Tap dance is so cool!"

Rupert Grint

RED-HAIRED cutie Rupert also plans to continue acting. He has been in a few non-Harry movies over the past couple of years. Rupert played a delivery-boy-turned-hitman in 2009's *Wild Target* with Helena Bonham Carter and Bill Nighy. Then he played a troubled Belfast youth in 2009's dark, coming of age story *Cherrybomb*. He chose *Cherrybomb* because "I really liked the whole relationship triangle thing between the three of them, and the fact that it was set in Belfast was really cool because usually, like, Belfast films are like all about religion and troubles and stuff like that — this one you don't get any mention of that at all," he told ICM.

Both films were a stretch for Rupert and a definite departure from Ron Weasley! Over the next few years, Rupert would like branch out further and try characters outside of his comfort zone. He'll miss playing Ron, but he's definitely ready to stretch his wings and see what he can really do with different types of roles! "…I think it's going to be quite weird when it's all over, because it has been such a massive part of my life. I think I'll miss it, in a way, but I am looking forward to freedom, really, when it's all over," he told *Time Out New York*.

Iron Man 2

Last summer, Robert Downey Jr. lit up the silver screen as ultra hero Iron Man. Now he's back to save the world again in *Iron Man 2* alongside fellow stars Scarlett Johansson, Samuel L. Jackson, Edward Norton, and Mickey Rourke! So how did Robert feel about stepping into Iron Man's shoes again?

Robert Downy Jr.

On playing Iron Man the second time around:

"The confidence was higher, but fun was not necessarily the word I would use to describe it. We felt more responsible to spend more time, and we had broadened our cast and horizons, and the story is actually significantly more complex and subtle—while you can still follow it. I don't want to say that it was as fun. It flew by, which was also odd, because we felt every punch, moment, laugh and everything last time. It was a really, really, really trying process to get this done to the best of our ability."

On donning the suit again:

"It was a little easier. Not enough for my taste."

On living up to expectations:

"I've never been in a sequel and it's very daunting because I feel the expectation of the millions of people who watched it and enjoyed it and told me that it was a little different than your usual genre picture and that they expected us to not screw it up. So

I actually have taken *Iron Man 2* probably more seriously than any movie I've ever done, which is appropriately ridiculous for Hollywood."

On taking risks for the sequel:

"The set pieces have to do with things that aren't your typical, like, bad guy conflict. The relationships are very complex and hilarious. The motivations Tony has and why he turns around and does things has completely to do with his own internal processes and it really is, I think, as much as we tried to in the first one really see behind the façade of this kind of storytelling. We're really, I think, leaving ourselves open to…we're kind of trying to tell a story about how a dysfunctional family saves life on Earth as we know it."

The Last Song

Miley Cyrus is shedding her Hannah Montana wig to star in a radically different movie. She will capture your heart as troubled teen "Ronnie" in this touching, coming of age story written by Nicholas Sparks. And you can bet the music will be rockin'!

The Last Song is based on a novel by Nicholas Sparks. He's the same author that gave the world *The Notebook* and *A Walk to Remember*—both very romantic movies! Miley has done a great job about keeping mum about *The Last Song* to the press, but she has let a few tidbits slip! She told MTV News that "I changed a lot when I was in Tybee Island [Georgia, filming *The Last Song*]. I feel like art really does imitate life. So just showing this movie, I feel like I'm really showing a part of my growth as a person as well. So I'm really excited for people to see it, just because of what it means to me, personally." Hmm….you'll have to wait to see the movie to figure out what Miley was talking about, but it sounds like one amazing movie! We can't wait to see how Miley tackles a complex role that is so different from Hannah! But we're pretty sure she's going to rock it!

MILEY SAYS:

MILEY CYRUS has had a lot of ups and downs over the past few years, but it seems like she is finally settling down and getting back to things that are most important to her. Miley has been playing Hannah Montana for a long time. As that part of her life comes to a close, she's really looking to branch out and try new roles. She's focusing on her music and defining her personal sound as Hannah falls away. So what's next for this adorable Southern belle? Movies, movies, and more movies if she has anything to say about it! Miley told a reporter at www.movies.ie, "I just want to continue to do film. You know, whatever it takes to do that. I loved doing my show, but film is what I really want to do. And I think that will be proven with my next movie." Well, her next film role is a doozy!

THE CHRONICLES OF NARNIA:
VOYAGE OF THE DAWN TREADER

Beautiful Brit actors Ben Barnes, Skander Keynes, and Georgie Henley are back for another adventure in Narnia. This time they will take to the high sea aboard the *Dawn Treader*. So how do cuties Ben and Skandar feel about starring in the epic Narnia series?

Ben Barnes

On getting into character as Prince Caspian:

"Well, I think the reason I like the character is because he's sort of an everyman. It's sort of a coming of age story, really. It's from boy-to-man and prince-to-king. . . . And obviously it's been adapted somewhat from how it is in the book because the kids that were in the first one have grown up so much that it's very hard to keep them as young children. So it all had to kind of grow up a little bit. But, hopefully, I think he's a kind of every-man character that you go on the journey with and sort of drags you through the story. Hopefully you kind of emphasize with him and latch on to what he's feeling and when he's feeling vulnerable, you feel vulnerable; and when he's feeling strong, you're feeling good about what's happening. So I think principally, he's that kind of character. But he's very honorable and those are kind of the principal things, really."

On the hectic training schedule to prepare for the role:

"Once I got to New Zealand I had a good few weeks. I literally got off the plane, and within 20 minutes of getting off the plane in New Zealand I was on a horse. And they were like, 'Okay, go.'

And I did it every day for two months, I think. I was riding with these fantastic Spanish horse trainers we've got and doing the stunt training with Allan Poppleton, who choreographs all the fights for us. He's fantastic. And so I had a good sort of eight weeks out there, whilst filming little bits and pieces, but I had a good eight weeks of quite hardcore training."

On working with CGI characters in the Narnia movies:

"…Actually, the first scene that I shot with a CGI character as with Trufflehunter, the badger. And the director, Andrew, has a wonderful assistant who's a fantastic actress as well. And so she just put on this completely lime green suit, balaclava, gloves, the whole everything, and was hobbling about on her knees, and she was holding the real props, like the actual tray that the badger will be holding. She was kind of putting it on the counter in this kind of – like a badger, and that's really easy to work with."

Skander Keynes

On the biggest challenges of filming the Narnia movies:

"One of the biggest challenges was sort of the step up in the physical aspect of the shoot. I was quite unfortunate because in one of my stunts I was running and jumping off this rock and landing on a horse. But one time, at the very beginning of all this action, I missed the horse, so I had a busted heel. It wasn't in a cast but it was really badly bruised and any time you put any weight on it, it hurt. So I had to do the rest of the battle sort of doped up on painkillers, which proved very problematic. It made it really difficult and made more of a challenge something that was already not a piece of cake."

On filming *The Voyage of the Dawn Treader*:

"I think it's going to be a completely different experience because we have a different director [Michael Apted] and that means a whole new crew and different actors. There was one point in the second film where we thought, 'well, it's one thing to have new people come on and the more the merrier, but now there's going to be a completely different set of ideas as people go away.' With that in mind, I think it's going to be weird, but at the end of the day it should be a great experience and hopefully I'll make the most of it."

PERCY JACKSON & THE OLYMPIANS: THE LIGHTNING THIEF

If you thought the Greek gods and goddess died out years ago, then you are in for a big surprise! In this movie based on the book of the same name, young Percy Jackson, played by Logan Lerman, discovers that he is the son of Poseidon, Greek god of the sea. After teaming up with other demigod teens, Percy sets out on a quest to keep Mount Olympus from being torn apart by war. Luckily, there are five books in the series so Logan and his cutie co-stars should be back from many more big-screen adventures!

Lots About Logan:

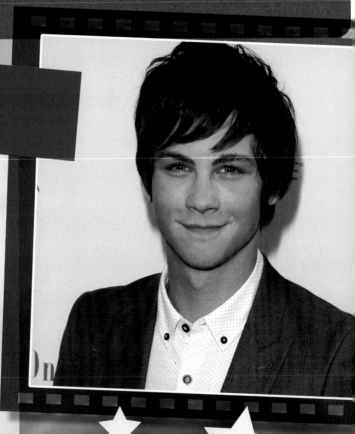

- Logan Lerman plays Percy Jackson in *The Lightning Thief*.
- His first big break was playing alongside Mel Gibson in *The Patriot* when he was only 8 years old.
- You probably know Logan from the movie *Hoot*.
- Logan is 18 years old. His birthday is January 19th.
- He plays soccer and baseball.
- His favorite sports team is the LA Lakers.
- His favorite way to spend his downtime is playing sports, watching classic movies, and making funny movies with his friends.

- Alexandra Daddario plays Annabeth Chase in *The Lightning Thief*.
- She got her start on the soap opera *All My Children*.
- Alexandra grew up in New York City.
- She went to an all-girls high school until her junior year.
- Alexandra got to play a bit part in *The Jonas Brothers: 3D Concert Experience*. She was part of the couple in Central Park!

The Best of
BRANDON:

- Brandon T. Jackson plays Grover Underwood in *The Lightning Thief*.
- He appeared in *Super Sweet 16: The Movie* alongside pop duo Aly & AJ.
- Brandon has 6 brothers and sister!
- Stand-up comedy is Brandon's true passion.
- Brandon grew up just outside of Detroit, Michigan.

Just
JAKE:

- Jake Abel plays Luke in *The Lightning Thief*.
- He has appeared in lots of TV shows including *The Suite Life of Zack & Cody!*
- Jake's favorite sports teams are the Cleveland Browns and the Cleveland Cavaliers.
- He has 2 dogs named Cooper and Maya
- Jake's favorite TV show is *Family Guy*.
- He grew up in the small town of Canton, Ohio.

Prince of Persia: The Sands of Time

Who says video games aren't quality entertainment? Hottie Jake Gyllenhaal and beautiful Gemma Arterton bring the *Prince of Persia* video game to life on the big screen. It's filled with cool settings, amazing costumes, and, of course, tons of awesome special effects! Here are all the facts you need to know about the film's biggest stars:

Jake Gyllenhaal

BIRTHDAY: December 19, 1980

HOMETOWN: Los Angeles, California

BIG BREAK: City Slickers

BIGGEST MOVIES: Zodiac, Jarhead, Proof, Brokeback Mountain, The Day After Tomorrow, The Good Girl, Donnie Darko

HEIGHT: 6'0"

HOBBIES: basketball, jogging, bicycling, cooking

PETS: a German Shepherd named Atticus and a Puggle named Boo Radley

FAVORITE BOOK: To Kill a Mockingbird

Gemma Arterton

BIRTHDAY: January 20, 1986
HOMETOWN: Gravesend, England
BIG BREAK: *Quantum of Solace*
BIGGEST MOVIES: *A Deal Is a Deal, RocknRolla, Pirate Radio, The Disappearance of Alice Creed*
HEIGHT: 5'7"
HOBBIES: field hockey

Ben Kingsley

BIRTHDAY: December 31, 1943
HOMETOWN: Scarborough, England
BIG BREAK: *Gandhi*
BIGGEST MOVIES: *The Love Guru; War, Inc.; The Wackness; The Last Legion; Lucky Number Slevin; Oliver Twist; Suspect Zero; Thunderbirds; House of Sand and Fog; Rules of Engagement; Species; Schindler's List; Searching for Bobby Fischer; Dave; Bugsy; The Assignment*
SPECIAL HONORS: Knighted by Queen Elizabeth II
HEIGHT: 5'8"
HOBBIES: reading, traveling, spending time with his 4 children

Ramona and Beezus

Anyone who's ever had to deal with a super-annoying sibling can relate to *Ramona and Beezus* starring Disney princess Selena Gomez and Joey King as two sisters who just can't seem to get along.

Selena Says:

On becoming famous:

"I started in this business because I love acting. I was ecstatic when I got *The Wizards of Waverly Place*. When we first started shooting it, we actually had to pay people to come and watch the show because no one knew what it was! Now we haven't even started season three and all of our shows are sold out. It's been really crazy, but it's been wonderful."

On her rise to fame:

"After *Barney*, I kept working steadily in commercials because that's all they really have in Dallas. Then the Disney Channel had a nationwide casting search, so I sent them my tape and two weeks later they flew me to California. It was the first time I'd ever been there."

On her amazing fam:

"I'm really lucky in that they support everything I do. My family is obviously a big consideration when it comes to my career. They're the ones who have had to take me to all my auditions. They have sacrificed a lot. I still live at home with my parents—in fact I'll probably be 30 by the time I finally move out!"

On being a normal teen:

"My mom really tries to find time for me to spend with my friends because that's a big part of growing up. I have my core group of friends form Dallas, and my cousin Priscilla; she travels with me a lot. And luckily, I've also met some lovely people in the business."

On being a "good" girl:

"Having had to work really hard to get where I am has a lot to do with it, but mostly it's my parents. I've never disobeyed them. I've always tried to listen to them and do my best to follow the rules since they obviously know what's best for me. Of course, I am 16, so there are times when I fight with them, but that's normal."

On being a role model:

"I do understand that there are a lot of little girls that look up to me. I love that; it's really wonderful. I realize that means I have to watch what I say and what I do, but I don't think that's any kind of pressure; it's part of the job. I love my fans and would never want to do anything to hurt them. I'm only 16, and I will make mistakes…but I will try to keep those mistakes to myself."

On her perfect date:

"Nice. My parents would have to like him. Educated. Someone who makes me laugh."

JUST JOEY:

On Beezus and Ramona:

"I play Ramona, the cool little sister of Beezus. Doing the movie is really great, I have a lot of fun, Selena is my sister in real life now, too, and I love her on *Wizards of Waverly Place*. Hutch is really cool, too, he is like my brother, he can play basketball really good and he is going to be a NBA star one day."

On her fave job so far:

"It was great to meet all the different actors I worked with but I had the most fun doing *Ice Age* because it's my favorite movie."

On her future career moves:

"I would like to be on the Disney Channel. Maybe I'll be in *Zeke and Luther* or *Wizards of Waverly Place*."

RED DAWN

This war thriller is not for the faint of heart! But it is full of hotties that will make your heart skip a beat! Cuties Chris Hemsworth, Josh Hutcherson, Josh Peck, Edwin Hodge, and Conner Cruise team up to save their Midwestern town from an invasion of Russian and Chinese soldiers during World War III. Here are the basic facts you'll need to know about these super hot co-stars!

Chris Hemsworth

BIRTHDAY: August 11, 1983

HOMETOWN: Melbourne, Australia

BIG BREAK: Kim Hyde on Australian television show *Home and Away*

BIGGEST MOVIES: *Star Trek, A Perfect Getaway, The Cabin in the Woods*

NEXT PROJECT: Thor in 2011's *Thor* and 2012's *The Avengers*

SIBLINGS: brothers and fellow actors Luke and Liam

HEIGHT: 6'3"

Josh Hutcherson

BIRTHDAY: October 12, 1992

HOMETOWN: Union, Kentucky

BIG BREAK: *The Polar Express*

BIGGEST MOVIES: *Bridge to Terabithia; Cirque du Freak; Journey to the Center of the Earth; Little Manhattan; Zathura: A Space Adventure; Kicking & Screaming*

NEXT PROJECT: *Journey to the Center of the Earth* sequel

SIBLINGS: younger brother Connor

HEIGHT: 5'6"

PETS: dogs Diesel and Baxter, cats Jell-O and Paws

Josh Peck

BIRTHDAY: November 10, 1986
HOMETOWN: New York City, New York
BIG BREAK: Nickelodeon's hit show *Drake & Josh*
BIGGEST MOVIES: *The Wackness; Drillbit Taylor; Ice Age: The Meltdown; Ice Age: Dawn of the Dinosaurs; What Goes Up; Aliens in the Attic; American Primitive*
HOBBIES: ice hockey, karate, beatboxing, stand-up comedy
HEIGHT: 6'1"
PETS: a dog named Monster

BIRTHDAY: January 17, 1995
HOMETOWN: Los Angeles, California
BIG BREAK: *Seven Pounds*
FAMOUS FAM: Adopted parents Tom Cruise and Nicole Kidman

Connor Cruise

Edwin Hodge

BIRTHDAY: January 26, 1985
HOMETOWN: Jacksonville, North Carolina
BIG BREAK: television show *Jack & Bobby*
BIGGEST MOVIES: *Die Hard with a Vengeance, The Long Kiss Goodnight, Big Momma's House*
NEXT PROJECT: *Young Americans*
SIBLINGS: brother and fellow actor Aldis Hodge

Remember Me

Super-hot Robert Pattinson steps away from his vampire ways to star as a troubled young man who falls in love with an equally troubled young girl. Their rocky romance is sure to bring a tear to your eye. After all, who wouldn't want to be in love with adorable Rob?

Robert Pattinson

TWILIGHT fans already know Robert makes one super-hot vampire, but Rob is looking to branch out beyond the supernatural. He took on troubled artist Salvador Dali in 2009's *Little Ashes*, which was a far cry from dreamy Cedric Diggory or mysterious Edward Cullen. In *Remember Me*, Rob really steps up as a romantic leading man. However, when it comes to his own love life, Rob isn't really ready to be a leading man just yet as he explained to *GQ* magazine! His busy schedule makes it tough to connect with any girls. "I don't see people. I don't even have people's phone numbers. I almost don't want to have a girlfriend, in this environment." Another big dating problem for the adorable star? Tabloids spreading false rumors about him! "There's this thing about my supposed girlfriend. There's this one girl who's consistently mentioned. It's like, 'He's dating this Brazilian model.' … I've never met her," Rob explained. It would probably be pretty tough to keep a girlfriend with rumors like that floating around all the time! Rob's ideal Miss Right would be just as low-key as he is. He loves to hang out at home or go out to small concerts. And he's very shy, especially on first dates! He hates awkward silences. "I just say the first thing that comes into my head out of nervousness," Rob admitted. But until the *Twilight* buzz dies down and Rob can go on a date without it ending up in magazines, he's planning on staying single. So don't worry, Rob fans—he won't be off the market anytime soon!

Emilie de Ravin

EMILIE was already the envy of girls around the world because of her gorgeous blonde curls, adorable Aussie accent, pretty face, and starring role on *Lost*, one of the hottest shows on television. But now she gets to play Rob Pattinson's love interest in *Remember Me*. How lucky can one girl get? Emile has been very picky about selecting movie roles. And she can afford to be! "I suppose it opens a lot more doors when you're on something very successful or involved with something very successful. You get a little more creative selection in what else you're doing. Again, I got to get involved with something that is so well-written and there are great actors involved," Emilie explained to About.com. But Emile jumped at the chance to star with hunky Rob. Plus, the role of Ally in *Remember Me* is very different from what she's been doing. And that's very important to Emile. She doesn't want to get locked into any stereotypes when it comes to acting roles, as she told About.com, "I think I'll continue working on projects that are all very different and unique. I like to be challenged by everything I do in a different way. Work on things I'm passionate about, with people I respect." Talented and smart? What more could Rob ask for in a co-star?!

Ridley Scott's Robin Hood

Robin Hood gets a darkly romantic make-over thanks to director Ridley Scott. With Russell Crowe as the ruggedly handsome Robin Hood and Cate Blanchett as the stunning damsel in distress Maid Marion, this movie is perfect for date night. It's packed with action and adventure for guys and plenty of romance for girls!

BIRTHDAY: April 7, 1964

HOMETOWN: Wellington, New Zealand

CURRENT HOME: Nana Glen, New South Wales, Australia

BIG BREAK: The Sum of Us

BIGGEST MOVIES: State of Play; American Gangster; 3:10 to Yuma; Cinderella Man; A Beautiful Mind; Proof of Life; Gladiator; The Insider; Mystery, Alaska; L.A. Confidential

NEXT PROJECT: The Next Three Days

HOBBIES: rugby, riding his motorcycle, singing, writing music

Russell Crowe

Cate Blanchett

BIRTHDAY: May 14, 1969

HOMETOWN: Melbourne, Australia

CURRENT HOME: Hunter's Hill, New South Wales, Australia

BIG BREAK: Elizabeth

BIGGEST MOVIES: The Curious Case of Benjamin Button; Indiana Jones and the Kingdom of the Crystal Skull; Elizabeth: The Golden Age; Babel; The Aviator; The Life Aquatic with Steve Zissou; The Lord of the Rings: The Return of the King; The Missing; The Lord of the Rings: The Two Towers; The Lord of the Rings: The Fellowship of the Ring

NEXT PROJECT: Indian Summer

Kevin Durand

BIRTHDAY: January 14, 1974
HOMETOWN: Thunder Bay, Ontario, Canada
BIG BREAK: Mystery, Alaska
BIGGEST MOVIES: X-Men Origins: Wolverine; 3:10 to Yuma; Wild Hogs; Smokin' Aces; Big Momma's House 2; The Butterfly Effect
TELEVISION WORK: Dark Angel, Lost
NEXT PROJECT: Legion
HOBBIES: reading, sports, writing
FAVORITE BAND: Great Big Sea
FAVORITE SPORT: ice hockey

BIRTHDAY: October 17, 1974
HOMETOWN: Great Yarmouth, Norfolk, England
BIG BREAK: The Reckoning
BIGGEST MOVIES: Pride & Prejudice, Death at a Funeral, Grindhouse, Frost/Nixon
TELEVISION WORK: MI-5

Matthew Macfadyen

Scott Grimes

BIRTHDAY: July 9, 1971
HOMETOWN: Lowell, Massachusetts
BIG BREAK: Critters
BIGGEST MOVIES: Crimson Tide; Mystery, Alaska
TELEVISION WORK: Who's the Boss?; ER; American Dad!
HOBBIES: writing music, singing
FAVORITE SPORT: ice hockey

The Tooth Fairy

Ever wondered what Dwayne "The Rock" Johnson would look like with a tutu and wings? Well, you can find out in *The Tooth Fairy*! Dwayne stars as a hockey player who is sentenced to serve time as a real-life tooth fairy after he destroys a child's dreams. This super-goofy comedy is sure to bring a big toothy grin to your face—whether you believe in the tooth fairy or not! Dwayne shared some of his thoughts about the hilarious movie.

ON PLAYING A FAIRY:

"Any time that I can put on a tutu with wings and have my magic fairy dust and collect teeth and have Julie Andrews as my fairy godmother and Billy Crystal as one of my other tooth fairies – It comes down to material. And you always look for good material that's going to entertain the audiences. I jumped at playing the Tooth Fairy because it's an opportunity to show the world, for the very first time, a movie about a character that's been around for centuries. And it reminds me of, like, *Miracle on 34th Street*, you know, where you introduced the world to Santa Claus or what our vision of the world of Santa Claus is going to be. This is our version of introducing the world to the Tooth Fairy."

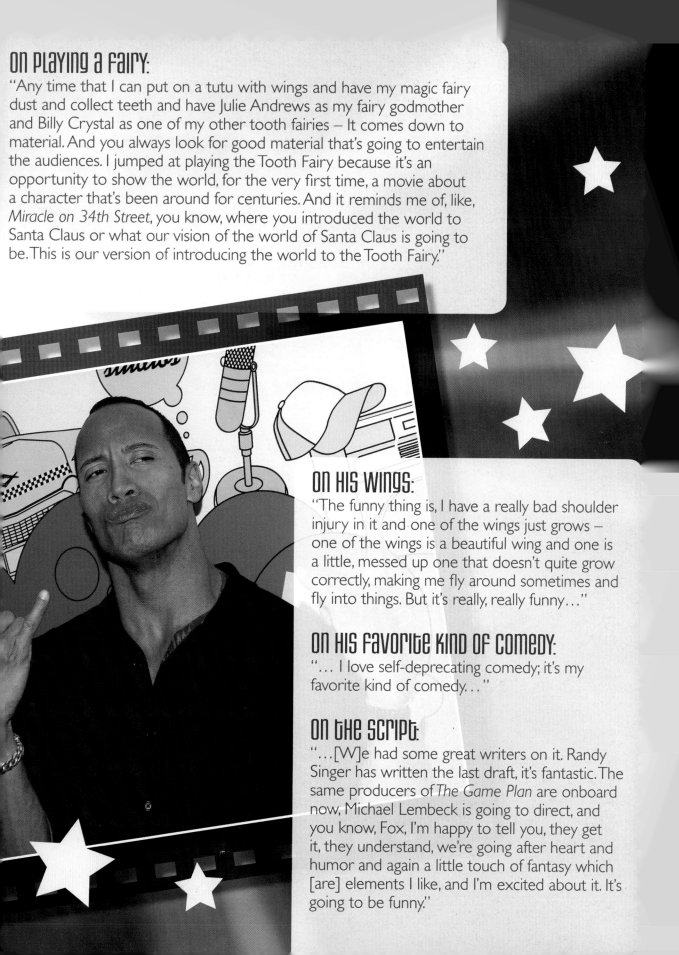

ON HIS WINGS:

"The funny thing is, I have a really bad shoulder injury in it and one of the wings just grows – one of the wings is a beautiful wing and one is a little, messed up one that doesn't quite grow correctly, making me fly around sometimes and fly into things. But it's really, really funny…"

ON HIS FAVORITE KIND OF COMEDY:

"… I love self-deprecating comedy; it's my favorite kind of comedy…"

ON THE SCRIPT:

"…[W]e had some great writers on it. Randy Singer has written the last draft, it's fantastic. The same producers of *The Game Plan* are onboard now, Michael Lembeck is going to direct, and you know, Fox, I'm happy to tell you, they get it, they understand, we're going after heart and humor and again a little touch of fantasy which [are] elements I like, and I'm excited about it. It's going to be funny."

YOUR HIGHNESS

Ever feel like a princess waiting for your Prince Charming? Then *Your Highness* is the movie for you. In this bawdy romantic comedy, an arrogant, lazy prince played by Danny McBride must complete a dangerous quest to save a beautiful princess played by Zooey Deschanel from an evil wizard. Adventure, danger, and super-hot princes? Sounds like a magical comedy indeed! So how do the film's two leading ladies feel about romance?

ZOOEY DESCHANEL
on love and heartbreak:

"Love can mean a lot of different things. The fear of losing it is the dark side, but the wonderful side is the feeling that you get when you fall in love. Everyone has the heartbreak that shapes them in a way that they could never go back to the innocence that they had before. It's beautiful and poignant and bittersweet to explore. That's why it is a universally appealing theme, because if you haven't been through this then you probably will go through it at some point."

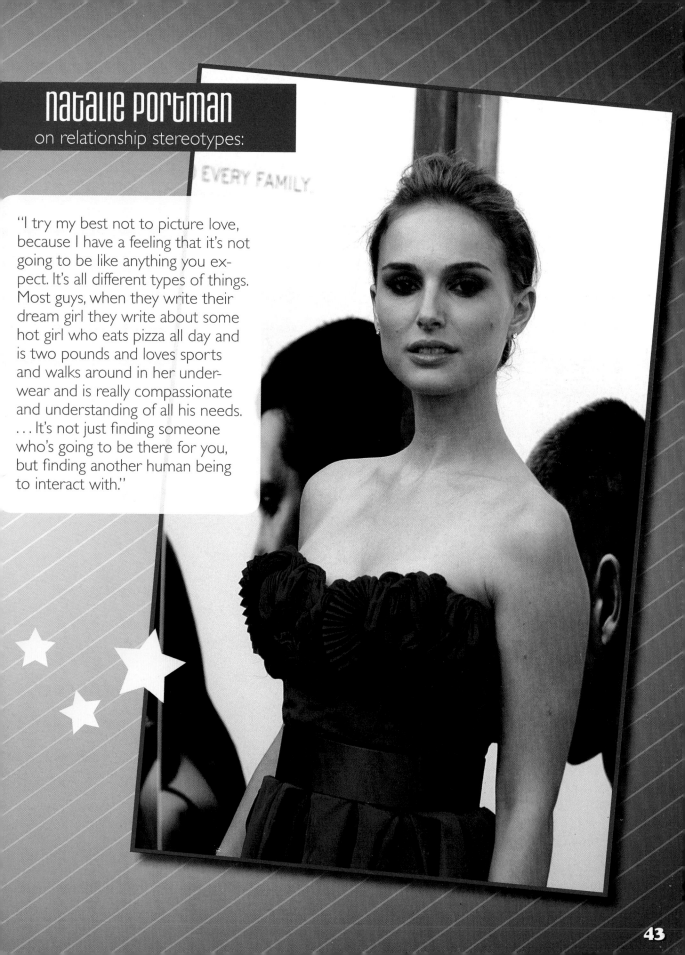

EVERY FAMILY

"I try my best not to picture love, because I have a feeling that it's not going to be like anything you expect. It's all different types of things. Most guys, when they write their dream girl they write about some hot girl who eats pizza all day and is two pounds and loves sports and walks around in her underwear and is really compassionate and understanding of all his needs. . . . It's not just finding someone who's going to be there for you, but finding another human being to interact with."

Getting Animated

Movie stars are known for their animated personalities—especially when they lend their voices to animated movies! Now get the low down on the biz straight from all your fave animated actors and actresses!

HAYDEN PANETTIERE
(Alpha and Omega)
"The biggest thing is just to surround yourself with good people who keep you driven and keep you going where you want to go. People who let you know that it's okay to be you."

CHRISTINA RICCI
(Alpha and Omega)
"I think to play somebody really well you should fully understand them, who they are, and what's happening to them."

JUSTIN LONG
(Alpha and Omega)
"The fact is, I love to work. I get very antsy when I'm not working. I just love acting and it's my favorite thing to do."

EMILIE DE RAVIN
(Guardians of Ga'Hoole)
"I'm very close with my family. They're very supportive of what I do and I'm very lucky to have that. I'm very close with my mum. She's supportive…And there's no way I could have moved to a different country unless I was working; I'm so close with my family, it would have been so hard. But when you're working everyday that it's put into the perspective, okay, I'm here and I'm working."

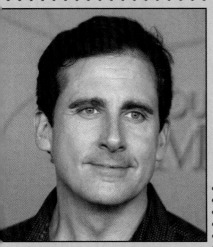

Steve Carell *(Despicable Me)*

"Comedy just sort of was a byproduct of what I was hired to do. Once I moved to Chicago and started trying to get acting jobs, I just tended to book more things that were comedically based than anything else. I never had the preconceived notion, 'I will be a comedic actor.' I just thought, 'I'll go into acting and see what kind of work I can get.'"

Miranda Cosgrove
(Despicable Me)

"It's so funny seeing your voice come out of an animated character and it's a comedy so it's been a lot of fun! They have been letting me come up with some of the lines and stuff and get really into it!"

 # Matt Prokop
(Furry Vengeance)

"Well, I was always kind of the class clown in school, and I just wanted to find the place where I wouldn't get in trouble for talking too much. So I started going to an acting class in Houston, Texas, and I went to an acting coach for about a year straight."

Jason Segel
(Despicable Me)

"Honestly, I don't know what it is, but I seem to have been born without a sense of shame or embarrassment, for the most part. Very few things make me feel uncomfortable…"

Hugh Jackman
(Guardians of Ga'Hoole)

"I work hard and I really enjoy it—I've always loved acting—but I can switch it off."

Brendan Fraser
(Furry Vengeance)

"I don't take myself too seriously. I think if you can treat comedy as normal then inevitably you will get more laughs. Even in adventure hokum you have to stick to the rules and parameters—then give the character a heart."

Gerard Butler
(How to Train Your Dragon)

"I don't know if I'm the best actor out there, but I definitely have how would you say? I have a lot of range."

america ferrera
(How to Train Your Dragon)

"When it comes to envisioning an actor in a role that they haven't seen them in, people in this business can be a little uncreative. No one is willing to take a gamble…It's been more about developing my own material, finding roles that I would like to play and figuring out a way to get those things made."

Jonah Hill
(How to Train Your Dragon)

"I find things that happened in real life to be the funniest—things that you observe instead of crazy abstract things, you know. So little social interactions that are uncomfortable, the smaller things are more funny to me, and I feel like why wouldn't you write about something that happened to you? Because funny, uncomfortable things happen to me multiple times a day, as far as feeling uncomfortable or out of place."

Brad Pitt
(Oobermind)

"As I've gotten older I've become aware that time is fleeting. I don't want to waste whatever I have left. I want to spend it with the people I love, and I want to do things that really mean something."

Will Ferrell
(Oobermind)

"When I graduated college, I just tried my hand at an open mic for stand-up comedy. [It] was something…something I always wanted to try…It was just a period of trying different things and I was having fun with it and I thought, 'Boy, if I got paid to do this, this would be fun.'"

TINA FEY (Oobermind)

"Every kid has something they're good at, that you hope they find and gravitate toward. This is my thing. I don't think I was supposed to be a gymnast and accidentally landed on this."

MANDY MOORE (Rapunzel)

"I'm getting older and, not that I want to do anything crazy or risqué or anything, I just want to challenge myself a little bit more in different ways. And I don't even know what that is right now but when those certain projects come to you and you read that script, you're like, 'That's it.'"

DAVID SCHWIMMER (Rapunzel)

"I've always been pretty energetic. I'm very goal oriented. My parents from a very young age raised my sister and I under a pressure to achieve. They're both attorneys. So good marks, getting through university, there was a huge emphasis and pressure to do well and keep going."

MIKE MYERS (Shrek Forever After)

"I loved the whole idea behind the [Shrek] story, which is that you're beautiful, so don't let other people tell you that you're not just because you don't look like the people in magazines. Or because you're not that weird ideal body image that's out there right now."

EDDIE MURPHY (Shrek Forever After)

"I'm in the comedy business. I'm all about the laugh."

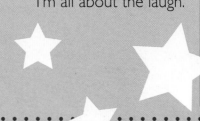

Tim Allen
(Toy Story 3)
"I enjoy movies, but I also enjoy movies that just aren't amusement park rides. I've seen a lot of big action films, and I don't know what they're doing. I don't know the purpose."

Tom Hanks
(Toy Story 3)
"Doing an animated voice is exhausting work. You're in a room and you're trying to create all of these verbal grunts and groans and also the energy that goes along with the character. You have to tax your psychic talents as well, because you have to see it all in your head and make it all up."

Adam Sandler
(The Zookeeper)
"I want to do more family-friendly movies now, as I feel good doing them. But, I know it's not going to be my way of life as I am a comedian."

Rosario Dawson
(The Zookeeper)
"I love playing women who are strong, and characters that have these great convictions and do the right thing. I'm always 100 percent behind that."